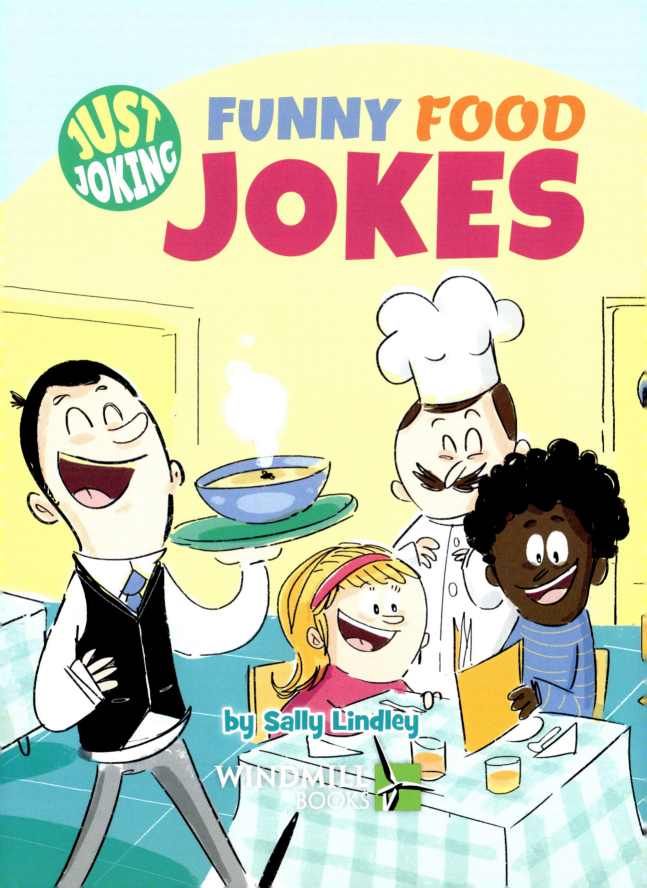

JUST JOKING

FUNNY FOOD JOKES

by Sally Lindley

WINDMILL BOOKS

Published in 2017 by Windmill Books, an Imprint of Rosen Publishing
29 East 21st Street, New York, NY 10010

Text: Sally Lindley
Illustrations: Fabio Santomauro
Design: Trudi Webb
Editors: Joe Fullman and Joe Harris

CATALOGING-IN-PUBLICATION DATA
Names: Lindley, Sally.
Title: Funny food jokes / Sally Lindley.
Description: New York : Windmill Books, 2017. | Series: Just joking | Includes index.
Identifiers: ISBN 9781508192602 (pbk.) | ISBN 9781508192541 (library bound) | ISBN 9781508192459 (6 pack)
Subjects: LCSH: Food--Juvenile humor.
Classification: LCC PN6231.F66 L563 2017 | DDC 818'.602--dc23

Manufactured in the United States of America
CPSIA Compliance Information: Batch #BS16PK: For Further Information contact Rosen Publishing, New York, New York at 1-800-237-9932

CONTENTS

DOPEY DINNERS

What's yellow, sweet, and is found in the jungle?

Tarzipan!

How did the French fries get engaged?

With an onion ring!

How did the joke about the peanut butter become so popular?

I guess it must have spread!

What do garbage collectors like to eat?

Junk food!

WHAT'S THE BEST THING TO PUT INTO A PIE? Your teeth.

What did the egg say to the whisk?

I know when I'm beaten!

What are the strongest vegetables?

Muscle sprouts.

Did you hear about the paranoid orange?

He always kept his eyes peeled for danger!

Which vegetable do dogs like best?

Collie-flower!

What did the fast tomato say to the slow tomato?

Come on, ketchup!

5

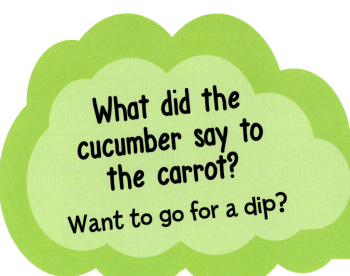

What did the cucumber say to the carrot?

Want to go for a dip?

Shakespeare walked into a diner and asked for a drink.

The man behind the counter shook his head and said, "You're Bard."

Why couldn't the farmer water his garden?

There was a leek in his bucket!

Knock knock!

Who's there?

Dishes.

Dishes who?

Dishes me. Who are you?

WHAT DO YOU GET IF YOU PUT THREE DUCKS IN A BOX?

A box of quackers!

Waiter, there's a snail in my salad!

That's okay, sir. Snails don't eat much.

What do you call shoes made out of bananas?

Slippers!

Why did dinosaurs eat raw meat?

They didn't know how to cook!

How do parrots drink?

Out of a beak-er!

Why shouldn't you put a lot of fungi in a stew?

Because there isn't mush-room!

Why won't you starve on a desert island?

Because of the sand which is there (sandwiches there).

If apples come from an apple tree, and oranges come from an orange tree, where do chickens come from?

A poul-tree.

What do you call a gingerbread man with a degree?

A smart cookie!

What did one knife say to the other?

Look sharp!

DID YOU HEAR ABOUT THE CANNIBAL WEDDING?

They toasted the bride and groom!

Why do monkeys like to eat bananas?

Because they have a-peel!

Which bird turns up at every mealtime?

A swallow!

What do you call cheese that belongs to someone else?

Nacho cheese!

What is green and sings?

Elvis Parsley!

What does a shark eat for dinner?

Whatever it wants!

WHAT DID ONE SNOWMAN SAY TO THE OTHER?

Can you smell carrots?

What do birds grow on?

Egg plants!

Knock knock!

Who's there?

Lettuce.

Lettuce who?

Lettuce in, and you'll find out!

Knock knock!

Who's there?

Carla.

Carla who?

Carla restaurant, I'm hungry!

Did you hear about the gravy that giggled?

It was made with laughing stock!

Why didn't the almonds go to the ballet?

Because they were afraid of The Nutcracker!

How do you make a walnut laugh?

Crack it up!

How do comedians like their eggs cooked?

Funny-side up!

Waiter, there's a dead fly swimming in my soup!

Don't be silly, madam. Dead flies can't swim.

What do you get if you cross a snake and an apple tart?

A pie-thon!

> # What did the cannibal order at the restaurant?
>
> Pizza with everyone on it!

What type of ice cream do birds like the most?

Chocolate chirp!

Where do baby cows go for lunch?

The calf-eteria!

What kind of dog doesn't have a tail?

A hot dog!

WHAT DO MONSTERS PUT IN THEIR SANDWICHES?

Scream cheese!

How do you fit an elephant in the fridge?

Open the door, and push it really hard!

How do you fit a giraffe in the fridge?

Take the elephant out first!

Why shouldn't you tease egg whites?

Because they can't take a yolk!

If you divide a marshmallow in half and then in half again, what do you get?

Really sticky fingers!

Why did the walnut go out with a raisin?

It couldn't find a date!

WHaT DiD SUSHi A say to SUSHi B?

"Wasabi?"
(What's up, B?)

Why did the truck driver stop for a snack?

He saw a fork in the road!

Why did the farmer work his field with a steamroller?

He wanted to grow mashed potatoes!

Why did the tofu cross the road?

To prove it wasn't chicken!

Why did the potato cry?

Someone had hurt its peelings!

Did you hear about the banana that went to charm school?

He turned into a real smoothie!

If you had 5 hens, 4 geese, and 6 ducks, what would you have?

Lots of eggs!

What would happen if pigs could fly?

The price of bacon would go up!

Why didn't the chef put herbs in the food?

He didn't have the thyme!

What does a penguin have in its salad?

Iceberg lettuce!

KOOKY KITCHENS

WHICH DRINK DO FROG'S ENJOY?

Croak-a-cola!

Knock knock!

Who's there?

Doughnut.

Doughnut who?

Doughnut ask, it's a secret.

Why was the mushroom invited to a lot of parties?

He was a fun-gi to be with!

What do you call someone who loves hot chocolate?

A cocoa-nut!

Which dessert is never on time?

Choco-late brownies!

What's white, sweet, and lives in the jungle?

A meringue-utan!

Why do seagulls fly over the sea?

Because if they flew over a bay, they'd be bagels!

Why did the gardener quit her job?

Because her celery wasn't high enough!

Which food do mathematicians like best?

Square-root vegetables!

Waiter, there's a twig in my meal!

Just a moment, sir, I'll get the branch manager.

WHERE DID THE SPAGHETTI GO TO DANCE?

To a meatball!

What kind of insect do you get if you throw butter out the window?

A butter-fly!

Which salad is the best at playing pool?

The cue-cumber!

What's orange and sounds like a parrot?

A carrot!

What did the nut say when it had a cold?

Cashew!

Did you hear about the numbskull who ate a light bulb?

He said he only wanted a light meal.

Knock knock!

Who's there?

Olive.

Olive who?

Olive just across the street from you.

What do mathematicians like to eat with their coffee?

Pi!

What do you call an egg that plays tricks on people?

A practical yolker.

What did the newspaper say to the ice cream?

Hey, what's the scoop?

Waiter, do you have frog's legs?

No, madam, I always walk like this.

Knock knock!
Who's there?
Figs.
Figs who?
Figs the doorbell. My hand hurts from all the knocking.

Knock knock!
Who's there?
Emma.
Emma who?
Emma going to have my dinner now?

What do you call a place with 8 million eggs?
New Yolk City!

Waiter, what is this spider doing on my ice cream?
I don't know, madam. Skiing, maybe?

Why shouldn't you ride to school on an empty stomach?

Because it's easier on a bicycle.

What does bread do after it comes out of the oven?

It loafs around!

Waiter, what's this?

It's bean soup, sir.

I don't care what it's been. What is it now?

Did you hear about the cabbage whose friend won the lottery?

He was green with envy!

What do you get if you cross a pig and a dinosaur?

Jurassic Pork!

What do you call a cheese that surrounds a castle?

Moat-zarella!

How does a penguin make pancakes?

With its flippers!

Teacher: Name four things that contain milk.

Student: Yogurt, butter, cheese, and... the truck from the dairy.

What vegetable are sailors scared of?

Leeks!

WAITER, THERE ARE FLIES IN MY SOUP!

Yes, sir, I think it's the rotten meat that attracts them.

What do you call a peanut in space?

An astro-nut!

Why did the farmer send his cows to the gym every day?

He wanted low-fat milk!

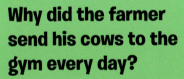

Why did the cook keep putting the peas through a colander?

He had a re-straining order!

Waiter, this lettuce tastes like soap.

I should hope so, madam, I just washed it.

Why did mother grape go on a spa retreat?

She was tired of raisin kids!

HOW DO YOU MAKE GOLDEN SOUP?

Put 24 carrots in it!

What kind of fruit has a bad temper?

A crab apple!

Waiter, do you serve lobsters here?

Yes, sir, we serve anybody.

Why did the chewing gum cross the road?

Because it was stuck to the chicken's foot!

What did the penguin order at the Mexican restaurant?

Brrr-itos!

Why did the teapot get in trouble?

Because it was naught-tea!

Why did the grape stop in the middles of the road?

He ran out of juice!

Teacher: Do you eat French fries with your fingers?

Student: No, I usually eat them with burgers.

Why did the man eat his lunch at the bank?

He loved rich food!

Why shouldn't you tell jokes to eggs?

Because they might crack up!

Waiter, there's a wasp in my soup!

I think you'll find it's a vitamin bee, sir.

What do cannibals eat for dessert?

Chocolate-covered aunts!

What do owls eat for breakfast?

Mice krispies!

Waiter, I think I just swallowed a fish bone!

Are you choking?

No, I'm serious!

WHAT DRINK DO SOCCER PLAYERS LIKE LEAST?

Penal-tea!

Where do milkshakes come from?

Dancing cows!

Why did the girl stare at the carton of juice?

Because it said "concentrate."

Where do cats prepare their meals?

The kit-chen!

What happened to the nutmeg that got arrested?

It ended up in custardy!

Where's the best place to store pizza?

In your stomach!

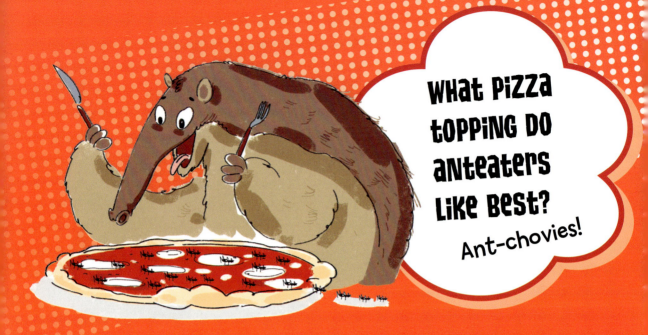

WHAT PIZZA TOPPING DO ANTEATERS LIKE BEST?

Ant-chovies!

Why do horses eat every day at the same time?

Because they need a stable diet!

Where do ice cream sellers learn their trade?

At Sundae school.

Why did the boy give mustard to his poodle when it had a fever?

Hot dogs are always better with mustard!

Why couldn't the sesame seed stop cracking jokes?

It was on a roll!

What do owls eat at the beach?

Mice cream!

When is the best time to pick apples?

When the farmer is away from home!

How do you get a mouse to smile?

Say cheese!

Why did the baker work overtime?

She kneaded the dough!

What did the bacon say to the tomato?

Lettuce get together!

Waiter, there's an ant in my soup!

I know, madam. The flies stay away during the winter.

How do you know that an elephant has raided your fridge?

There are footprints in the cheesecake!

Why didn't the large man know he was overweight?

It just kind of snacked up on him!

What do they eat at birthday parties in heaven?

Angel food cake!

WHAT KIND OF KEY OPENS A BANANA?

A mon-key!

Waiter, what is this fly doing in my soup?

Madam, it looks like the backstroke.

What do you say to bees who try to steal honey?
Oh, beehive yourself!

Which hotel do mice stay in?
The Stilton!

Waiter, there's a slug in my salad!
Don't worry, sir, we won't charge extra.

Did you hear about the angry pancake?

It just flipped!

CHUCKLESOME CHEFS

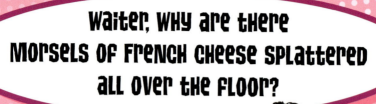

Waiter, why are there morsels of French cheese splattered all over the floor?

It's de Brie, sir.

What do dogs eat at the movies?
Pup-corn!

Why did the pig kidnap the farmer?
To save his own bacon!

What meal do atomic scientists like best?
Nuclear fission chips!

Waiter, I can't eat this food. Please call the manager.
It's no use, madam, he can't eat it either.

Why did the farmer think the chicken had stolen his dinner?

He suspected fowl play!

What kind of people eat snails?

Ones who don't like fast food!

Why did the baker stop making doughnuts?

He was bored of the hole business!

What do you call someone that takes her own salt and pepper everywhere she travels?

A seasoned tourist!

What's the worst thing about being an octopus?

Washing your hands before dinner.

What should you do if your chicken smells funny?

Don't eat it, it's fowl!

Why won't an oyster and a scallop share their food with each other?

Because they are two shellfish!

Why did the boy eat a cupcake each night before bed?

So he could have sweet dreams!

What's a dog's top sweet treat?

Pup-tarts!

WHAT KIND OF CHEESE DO YOU USE TO LURE A BEAR AWAY?

Camembert! ("Come on bear!")

Which day of the week do eggs hate?

Fry-day.

Waiter, there is a spider on my plate. Call the manager at once!

That won't do any good, sir. She's afraid of them, too.

What did the martial artist buy from the butcher?

Karate chops!

What did the cannibal say when he saw people running a marathon?

Yummy, fast food!

When are you allowed to take bubblegum to school?

On chews-day!

WHAT DO YOU CALL A REALLY LARGE PUMPKIN?

A plumpkin!

What do snowmen eat for breakfast?

Frosted flakes!

How can you spell the name of a hungry insect using just three letters?

M. T. B.

Why don't people laugh at gardeners' jokes?

Because they're too corny!

When should you take a cookie to the doctor?

When it feels crummy!

Where do tomatoes hang out on Fridays?

The salad bar!

Why did the chef dream that his pillow was turkey?

Because they're both full of stuffing!

What do farmers wear to gather their crops?

A har-vest!

Why did the banana go to see the doctor?

Because it wasn't peeling well!

WHY COULDN'T THE TEDDY BEAR FINISH ITS LUNCH?

Because it was stuffed!

A cheeseburger walks into a diner and asks for orange juice.

The waiter says, "I'm sorry, we don't serve food here."

What do you get if you keep your toys in the fridge?

A teddy brrrrr!

What's the difference between roast beef and pea soup?

Anyone can roast beef, but have you ever tried to pea soup?

What's the difference between ice cream and milk chocolate?

Anyone can scream, but no one can milk chocolate.

Are carrots really good for your eyesight?

Well, have you ever seen a rabbit wearing glasses?

What do vegetarian spiders eat?

Corn on the cobweb!

What do you call a spaceship made out of herbs?

A thyme machine!

How many more times do I have to tell you to walk away from the cupcakes?

None, I've eaten them all now!

Why did the fisherman put peanut butter into the sea?

To go with the jellyfish!

Why did the basketball player always have cookies with his drink?

So he could dunk them!

Did you hear about the hilarious banana?
It had the whole fruit bowl in peels of laughter!

Knock knock!

Who's there?

June.

June who?

June know what time dinner is?

Why did the baker get fired from her job?

She was a loafer!

What starts with "T," ends with "T," and is full of "T"?

A teapot!

WHAT CAN YOU SERVE BUT NEVER EAT?

Tennis balls!

Why did the turkey join a band?

He had his own drumsticks!

Knock knock!

Who's there?

Ken.

Ken who?

Ken you get me something to eat? I'm starving.

Where do fish eat their dinners?

At a water table!

How do you make an apple turnover?

Push it downhill!

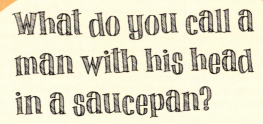

What do you call a man with his head in a saucepan?

Stu!

WHAT DID THE CAVEMAN ORDER FOR LUNCH?

A club sandwich!

How do you make a strawberry shake?

Put it in the freezer!

What did the spider order at the fast food restaurant?

A burger and flies!

Which fruit do twins like best?

Pears!

Did you hear about the cat that ate a lemon?

It was a sour puss!

Did you hear about the peanut who kept picking fights?

He was a-salted!

Waiter, there's a dead fly in my soup!
Sorry, madam, are you a vegetarian?

Why did the sausage roll?
Because it saw the milk shake!

What do astronauts eat out of?
Satellite dishes!

No, seriously, what do astronauts use to eat out of?
Flying saucers!

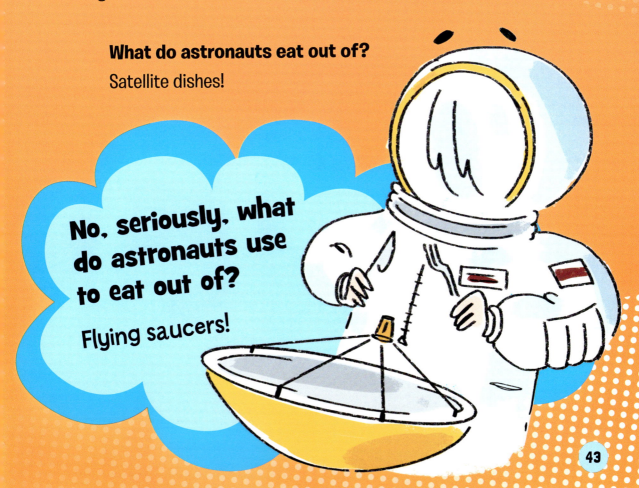

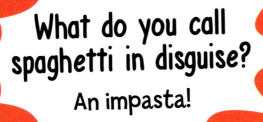

What do you call spaghetti in disguise?

An impasta!

Waiter, this food tastes funny.

Then why aren't you laughing?

Waiter, is there pizza on the menu?

No, madam, I just wiped it off.

Knock knock!

Who's there?

Annie.

Annie who?

Annie chance of getting something to eat?

WHAT ARE LARGE, HAVE HORNS, AND GIVE MILK?

Dairy trucks!

What did the plate say to the bowl?

Dinner is on me!

What did the baker say to the bread dough that tried to run away?
Stop, I knead you!

Waiter, will my pizza be long?
No, madam, it will be round.

Waiter, there's a dead fly in my soup!
Yes, sir. It looks like it committed insecticide.

Which drink do martial artists like the best?

Kara-tea!

WHY DiD THe GRaPe TrY NOt to SNOre?

It didn't want to wake up the rest of the bunch!

What happened to the cannibal who was late for lunch?

She got the cold shoulder!

Knock knock!

Who's there?

Justin.

Justin who?

Justin time for dinner.

How did the chef know that the oregano and basil would keep his secret?

Because only thyme will tell!

What did the baby corn say to its mother?

Ma, where's Pop corn?

What did the mayonnaise say to the refrigerator?

Close the door, I'm dressing!

Why did the spy hold his plate very carefully?

He didn't want to spill the beans!

What do computer experts like to snack on?

Micro-chips!

What's the difference between an elephant and a grape?

A grape squashes if you sit on it!

What's small, round, white, and giggles?

A tickled onion!

Further Reading

MacIntyre, Mickey. *The REALLY Funny KNOCK! KNOCK! Joke Book for Kids.* Bell & Mackenzie Publishing, 2014.

National Geographic Kids. *Just Joking: 300 Hilarious Jokes, Tricky Tongue Twisters, and Ridiculous Riddles.* National Geographic Kids, 2012.

Weitzman, Ilana. *Jokelopedia.* Workman, 2013.

Glossary

cannibal Someone who eats other people.

chef The main cook in a restaurant or café.

colander A piece of kitchen equipment with holes in it. It is used for straining food, such as pasta.

engaged When two people promise to marry one another.

garbage collectors People who take away garbage from households.

shallot A type of small onion.

waiter Someone who works in a restaurant or café, taking customers' orders and bringing them their food.

Index